How to

Train a Train

JASON CARTER EATON

ILLUSTRATED BY JOHN ROCCO

CANDLEWICK PRESS

So you want a pet train? Well, of course you do!
Trains make awesome pets—they're fun, playful, and extremely useful.
Lucky for you, this handy guidebook contains everything you need
to know to choose, track, and train your very own pet train.

Ready? Then let's head out and find some trains!

Different trains live in different places.

Freight trains live in the countryside and travel in herds.

Monorail trains live in the city and travel alone.

Early steam engines pretty much just sit in museums.

Have you decided which sort of train you'd like? Great.

Now you need to catch one.

There are lots of ways to catch a train. Some people will corner it.

Others might use a big net to trap it.

Still others will run the track into quicksand.

True, these methods all work.

But I'm going to show you
the *best* way. . . .

First, get up really early in the morning and find a good hiding spot close to some trains.

Now the hard part:

sit quietly and wait   and wait   and wait some more.

As the sun rises, the trains
will begin to stir and start their engines.
Watch them work and play.

It's only natural that you'll want to take home all the trains,
but don't just grab the first one you see.

Take your time and choose one that's right for *you*.

Got one? Time to make your move:
send a puff of smoke high into the air.

Perfect! You've got the train's attention!

If you brought any coal with you,
now would be the time to offer it.

Try saying,
"My, what a handsome train you are."

Next, make the call of the wild train:

CHUGGA-
CHUGGA,
CHUGGA-
CHUGGA!

Well done!
Here it comes!

How will you know if the train you caught is THE ONE?

Don't worry. You'll know.

Once you get your train home, you'll want to give it a name.
Some popular train names are:

MILO

MORGAN

NATHAN

PUSHKIN

SMOKEY

PICKLEPUSS

CAPTAIN FOOFAMALOO

LITTLE MISS MUFFINHEAD

SIR CHUGGSALOT

Don't worry if it seems shy or scared at first.
A train needs time to adjust to new surroundings.

A warm bath can help calm a nervous train . . .

and few trains can resist a good read-aloud.

If your train has trouble falling asleep at night, play soft locomotion sounds:

Rocka-rocka, clickety-clack! Rocka-rocka, clickety-clack!

This is an old conductor's trick that'll give your train good dreams.

Spend as much time as you can getting to know your train.

Does it prefer going fast or slow?

Does it like to fetch?

How does it feel about tunnels and bridges?

Want to teach your train a few tricks? Easy as pie!

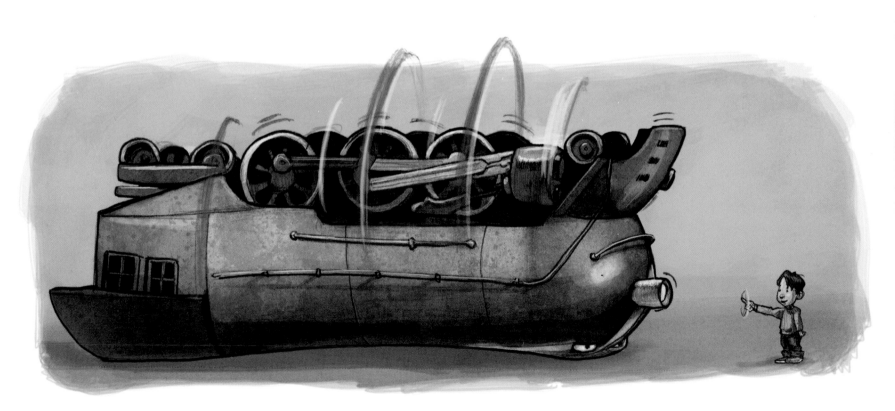

Start with a simple trick . . .

then move on to something a bit harder.

By now your train should be willing
to let you go for a ride.

But start out slow — try riding in the caboose at first.
(Trains are very particular about who sits in the engineer's car.)

Good manners are important.

Train your train not to leap up on people
and to always wipe its wheels
before going indoors.

Of course, your train can't go *everywhere* with you.

Out on the open road, you're sure to pass other kids
with *their* pet trains, planes, trucks, or submarines.

This is a great chance for both of you
to make new friends.

Congratulations!

You've given your train fuel, water, a good home,
and plenty of friendship and fun—
everything it needs to be happy.

How will you know if your train is happy?

FOR MILO
AND MORGAN,
MY OWN LITTLE
CONDUCTORS OF
INSPIRATION
J. C. E.

TO MY DAD
J. R.

Thanks to: Lisa Fragner for being the best wife and co-adventurer in the world, Mom and Dad for not making me go to law school, Mary Lee Donovan for the old-school genius, Tanya McKinnon for the mind-blowing magic, Ian Lendler for the always great advice, Karen and Bryant for the nerd love, Charlie Schroder for the good times, and David Marinoff for the good luck. —J. C. E.

Dear Readers (and the grown-ups who care about them),
While the author believes that it would indeed be wonderful to track, own, and train one's very own train, he does not suggest that you make a practice of standing in the middle of train tracks. Just as he does not suggest swimming in a train's bathtub without adult supervision, or traveling to the desert without an adequate water supply and SPF 1000 sunblock, or building a fire by yourself, or operating a train without the proper paperwork, or disobeying traffic laws, or walking across a train trestle several thousand feet up from the ground. All of these things are extremely dangerous and should be performed only by fully trained illustrated characters.